MAX SPEED

STEPHEN SHASKAN

Simon & Schuster Books for Young Readers
New York London Toronto Sydney New Delhi

SIMON & SCHUSTER BOOKS FOR YOUNG READERS
An imprint of Simon & Schuster Children's Publishing Division
1230 Avenue of the Americas, New York, New York 10020
Copyright © 2016 by Stephen Shaskan
SIMON & SCHUSTER BOOKS FOR YOUNG READERS is a trademark of Simon & Schuster, Inc.
For information about special discounts for bulk purchases, please contact Simon & Schuster Special Sales
at 1-866-506-1949 or business@simonandschuster.com.
The Simon & Schuster Speakers Bureau can bring authors to your live event. For more information or to book an
event, contact the Simon & Schuster Speakers Bureau at 1-866-248-3049 or visit our website at
www.simonspeakers.com.
Book design by Stephen Shaskan
The text for this book was set in Helvetica.
The illustrations for this book were rendered digitally.
Manufactured in China
0716 SCP
First Edition
10 9 8 7 6 5 4 3 2 1
Library of Congress Cataloging-in-Publication Data
Names: Shaskan, Stephen, author.
Title: Max speed / Stephen Shaskan.
Description: 1st edition. | New York : Simon & Schuster Books for Young Readers, [2016] | Summary: "Tiny speedcar racer, Max, goes on the
imagined adventure of a lifetime after cleaning his room—over hot lava, across bright blue skies, through shark-infested waters, and past super-
secret doors—until he finds his way back home to his mom . . . and the mess he made of his bedroom"— Provided by publisher.
Identifiers: LCCN 2015025636| ISBN 9781481445900 (hardcover) | ISBN 9781481445917 (eBook)
Subjects: | CYAC: Imagination—Fiction. | House cleaning—Fiction.
Classification: LCC PZ7.1.S4855 Max 2016 | DDC [E]—dc23 LC record available at http://lccn.loc.gov/2015025636

Dedicated to my grandma,
Helen Hoffmann

Max finished cleaning his room just in time for an adventure!

Max leaped into his super-secret car, waved good-bye to his mom, and zoomed off.

VA-ROOM-
A-ROOM-
ROOM!

What was that up ahead?
Something was blocking the road.

Oh no! It was a river of . . .

HOT LAVA!!!

SCREEEEEEEEECH!

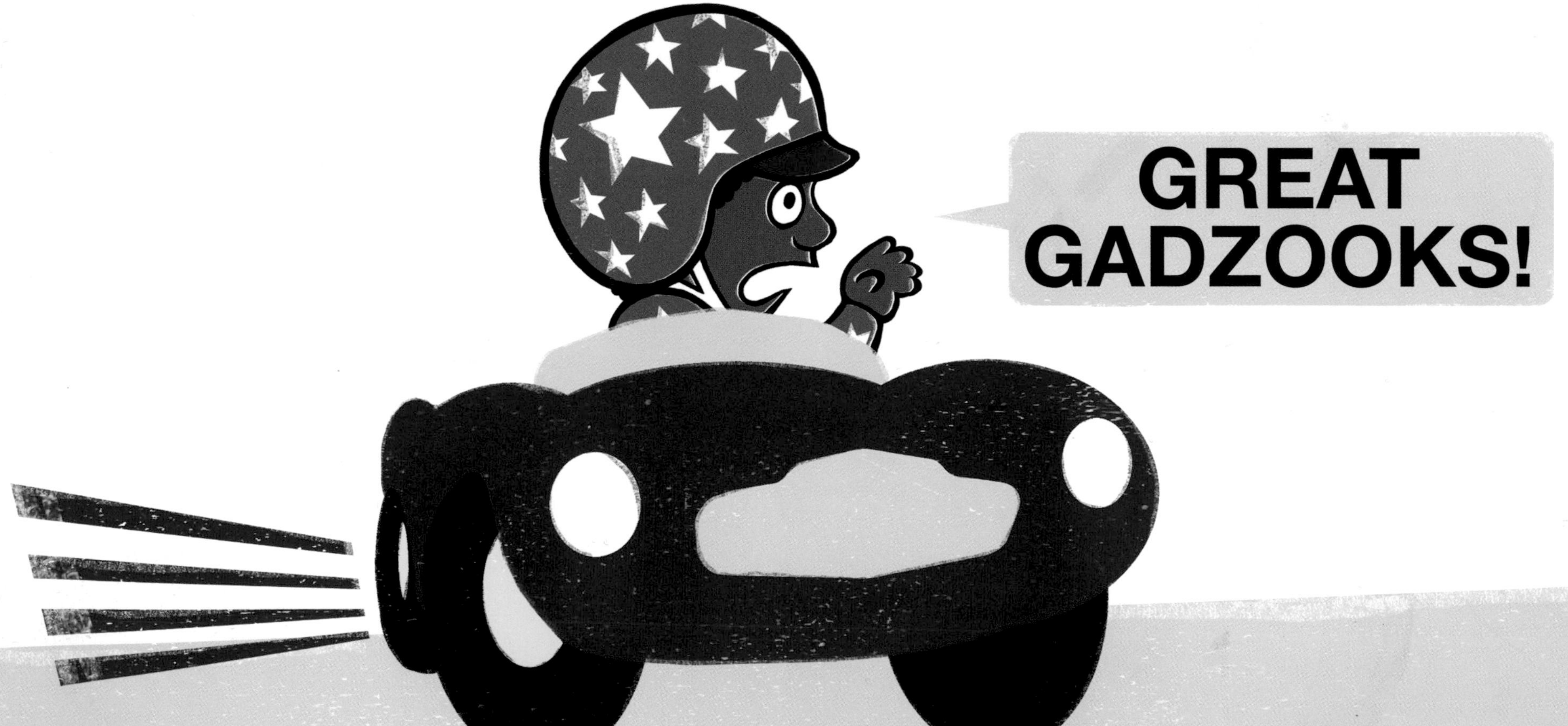

Had Max met his match?

Just in time, Max grabbed his super-secret jet pack.

WHOOOOOOOO

Max soared high above the hot lava.

Just in time, Max activated his super-secret parachute.

POOF!

Max
fell
gently
down
into . . . .

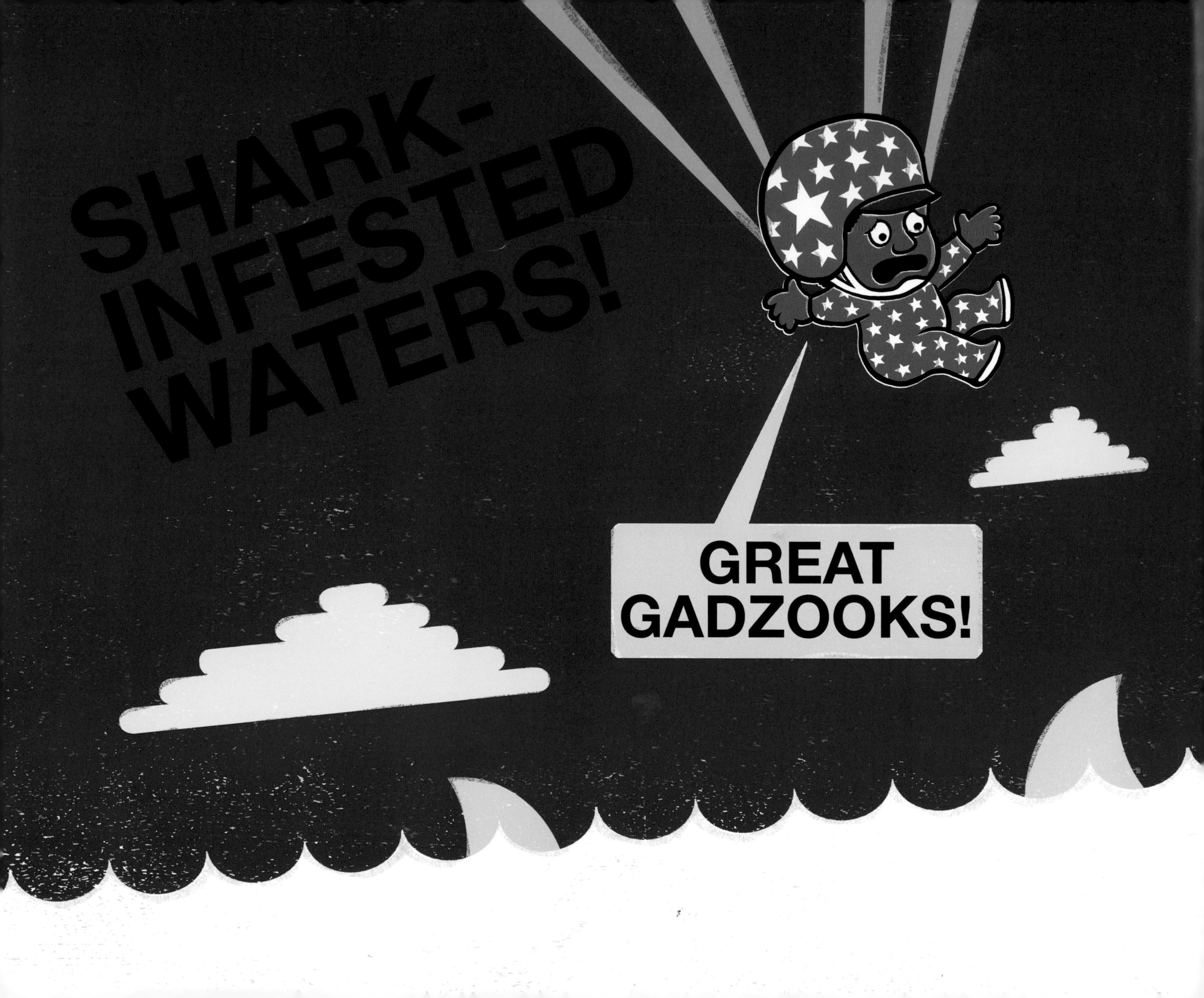
SHARK-INFESTED WATERS!
GREAT GADZOOKS!

Had Max met his match?

Just in time, Max spoke his super-secret shark language.

Sharky-shark-shark. Shark, shark-shark, sharky-shark. Shark, shark?

The sharks showed Max the way to
the super-secret underground cave.

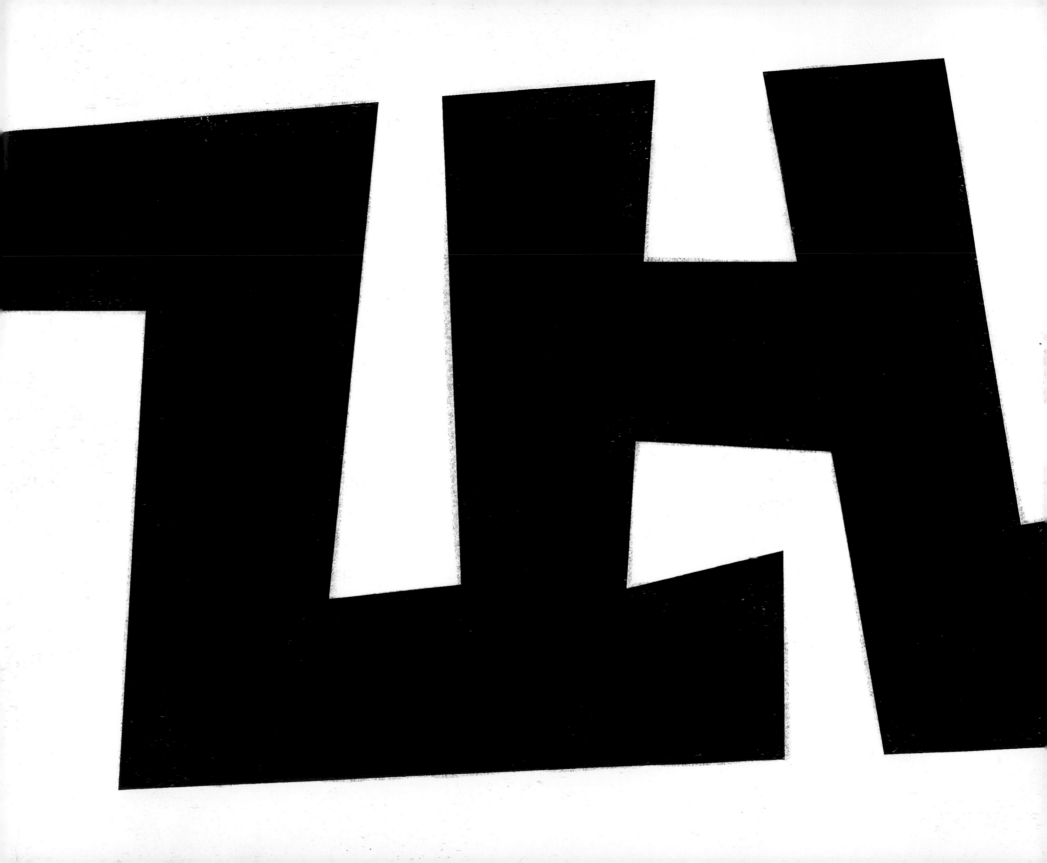

Max swam and swam until
he came to a dead end.

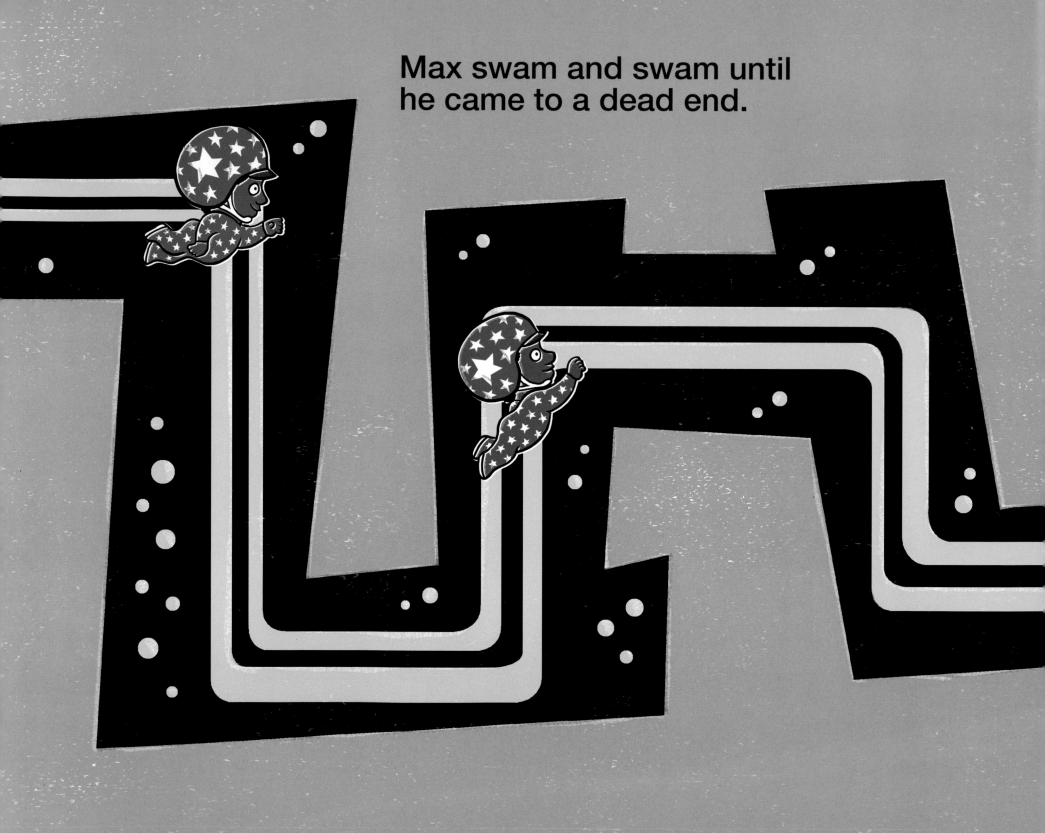

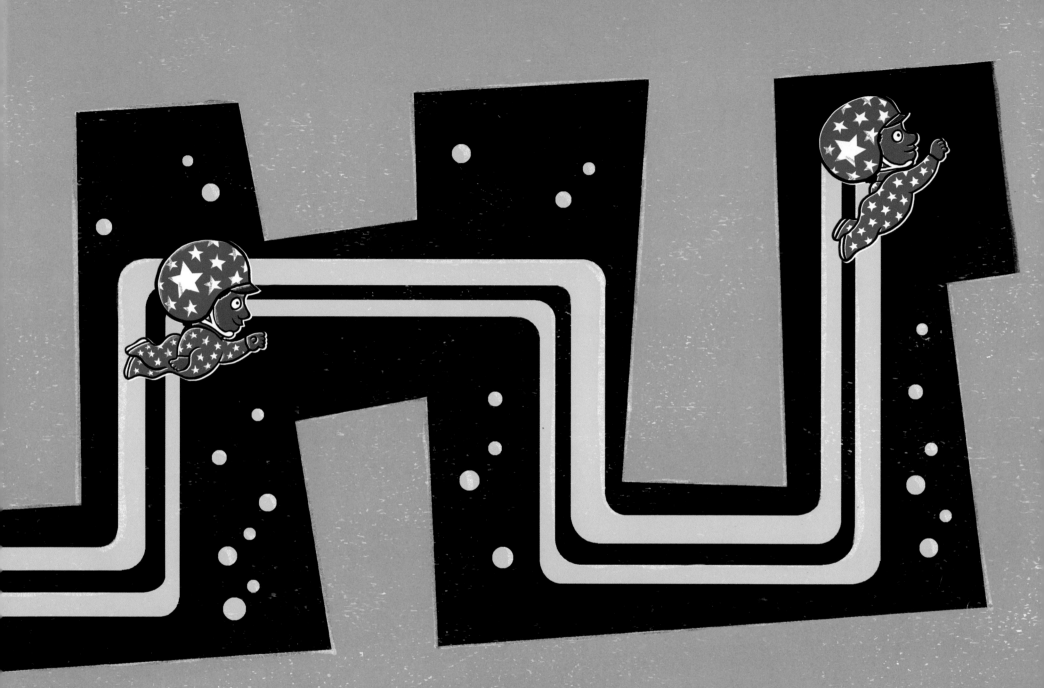

At that dead end there was a . . .

super-secret door with a super-secret combination!

Max was running out of time. He couldn't think fast enough. He couldn't even yell, "GREAT GADZOOKS!"

Had Max met his match?

Max thought about his toys, he thought about his room, and he thought about his mom.

Just in time, Max figured out the super-secret combination.

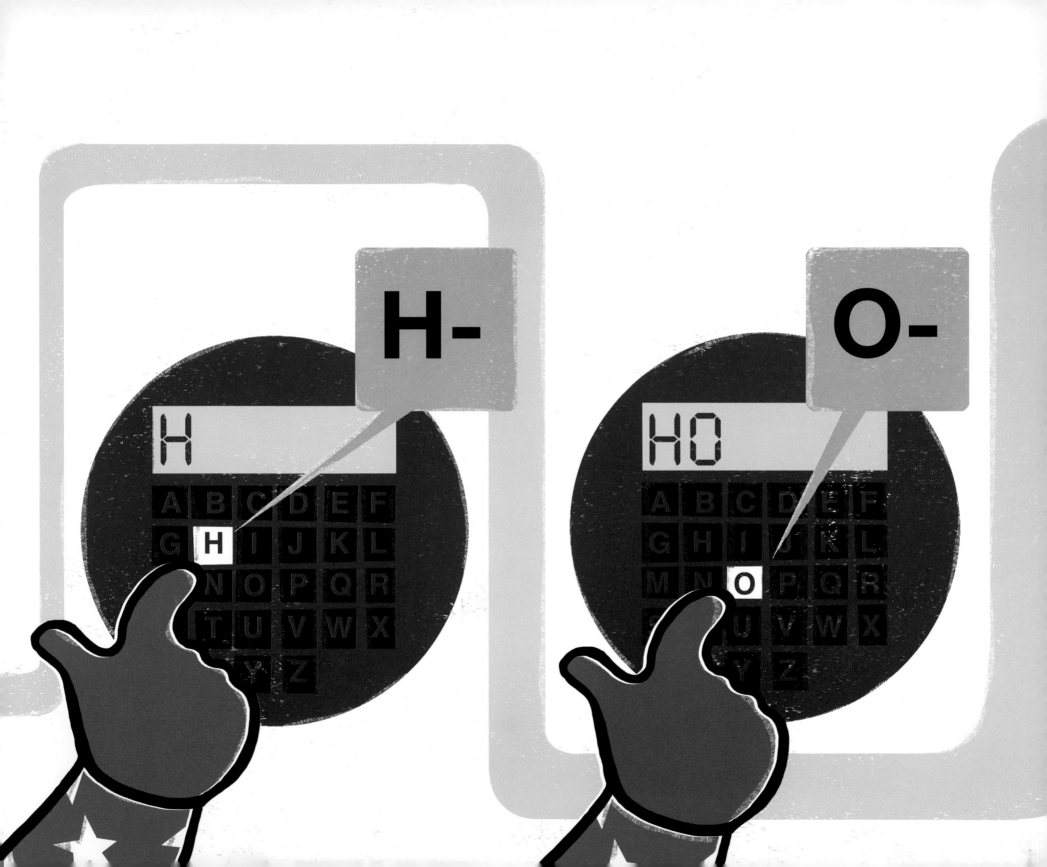

Max had finally met his match.